Keeping it Cool

10 humorous and uplifting short stories

Stefania Hartley

ALSO AVAILABLE IN
EBOOK AND LARGE PRINT

ISBN: 978-1-914606-53-3

"Old Bike, New Tricks" was never published before. "A Mother's Work" was first published in *My Weekly* magazine. The other stories were first published in *The People's Friend* magazine.

Edited by Sandy Salisbury

Cover illustration and design by Joseph Witchall
https://josephwitchall.com/

To Francesca.

CONTENTS

1. ONE OF A KIND

Mario didn't mind having a famous name. Mario Rossi was the everyman's name in Italy, like John Smith or Joe Bloggs in the English-speaking world.

Mario loved reading about his namesake's antics in Italian language textbooks, and was always thrilled to see his name on official documents, where it worked as a placeholder for the actual person's name.

"When I look at your ID card, I forget that it's your real one and not just a standard sample," his wife Claudia teased him.

"As long as you remember that our marriage certificate is real," he joked back.

Sometimes his name was considered suspicious. Once, querying an electricity bill, he was asked for a copy of his ID. When he renewed his driving licence, he was asked to repeat his name three times. But, apart from these times, being Mario Rossi had never given him any problems.

***

Roberta sat in her chair at reception and leafed through the newspaper, as she did every morning.

She always started with the obituaries because it made her feel more grateful for the day ahead. Today, one name caught her attention. Mario Rossi.

Her husband had a friend called Mario Rossi. They hadn't spoken for a while, after falling out over an electric screwdriver that Antonio had lent Mario and never got back.

She read the full obituary. It sounded like Antonio's friend. How dreadful that Mario had died before they'd had a chance to reconcile!

Roberta picked up her phone and called Antonio.

"Your friend Mario is dead. It's in today's paper," she announced as soon as Antonio picked up.

"That's sad. I shouldn't have got upset with him about that screwdriver. I don't think he remembered borrowing it from me. He is—was—always a bit of a scatterbrain. I should have just asked for my screwdriver back. Now it's too late."

"Too late to get your screwdriver back?"

"No. To make peace with Mario."

***

Looking after the obituary page of the local newspaper wasn't the most glamorous of publishing jobs, but it was Sabrina's first one, and a foot in the door.

Her dream was to write the culture and fashion pages, reviewing movies and trends, shoes and handbags. One day.

Right now, she collated names, ages and obituary messages and entered them into a spreadsheet. Then she transferred them onto the page template. Copy and paste, copy and paste, until all the placeholder text had been replaced by the real copy.

When she finished, she checked it, clicked *send*, and returned to dreaming about handbags and shoes.

***

Gabriele was driving home when his phone rang through the stereo system.

"Hello?"

"Gabriele, it's Antonio. Has anyone told you the news?"

"What news?"

"Mario passed away."

"Mario Rossi? I met him in at the park the other day and all that was wrong with him was a dodgy back."

Mario's dog had been barking, and Gabriele had asked Mario why he didn't throw its ball so that it could let off some steam. That was when Mario mentioned a bad back. Mario had always been on the lazy side, and Gabriele had thought that it was just an excuse.

What if it wasn't? Guilt washed over Gabriele.

"Poor Mario, he was a nice guy. It's so sad. How did it happen?"

"I don't know, but the obituary asks to refrain from visits, so I'm not going to bother his family."

"When's the funeral?"

"On Saturday at San Giuseppe's church."

"I'll tell the others."

***

Francesco was watching TV when his phone rang. The display showed that it was Gabriele.

"It's so nice to hear from you after such a long time!" he answered cheerfully.

"I wish I was calling for happier reasons. Mario has passed away."

"No! really?"

"I know. I met him only the other night when he was walking his dog," Gabriele replied.

That dog had bitten Francesco on the leg once, and Mario had never apologised. Mario didn't do apologies. But now that he was dead, Francesco didn't feel angry with him anymore.

In fact, quite the opposite. Suddenly, a warm feeling of tenderness and nostalgia bloomed in his heart for his friend. Poor Mario had been a good fellow. He had never been forthcoming to help others, but that was because he minded his own business and didn't poke his nose in other people's affairs. He wasn't weak; he was gentle. Okay, his terrible dog was out of control, but that was because Mario was too kind to discipline him. Poor Mario was a gentle soul. Francesco could have cut him more slack, but now it was too late.

***

Mario had just got home from work when the doorbell rang. He couldn't be bothered to answer it, so ignored it. Claudia would surely go.

"Look, Mario, we've received flowers!" Claudia announced, carrying a pillow of white and purple chrysanthemums.

It had a certain funereal look about it.

"Are you sure it's for us?"

"The card says: *For the Rossi family*, but I can't read who it's from. Water has smudged the ink."

"The florist will know," Mario said, hoping Claudia would get the hint and call the shop in the morning.

The following morning, more flowers arrived. This time, as well as pillows of chrysanthemums, there were wreaths, hearts and crosses. The senders' names weren't smudged: *Gabriele, Francesco, Antonio*. Why were his friends sending funeral flowers?

Mario picked up his phone and called.

***

Thirty of them turned up outside the church, but there was no sign of any funeral happening soon. In fact, the church was closed.

"Is this the right church?" Gabriele asked.

Antonio produced the newspaper's obituary page.

"Yes. Maybe the time is wrong."

They checked the page again. The time was right.

"Look at this." Francesco pointed to the obituary and frowned at what he read. "Mario wasn't a grandfather or a brother!"

Just then, Gabriele's phone rang. He pulled it out of his pocket, looked at the screen and gasped. The call was from the dead man's number.

***

"Who's that?" Gabriele answered in a shaky voice.

"Don't you have my number in your

phone's memory?" Mario replied.

He immediately regretted it because it wasn't fair to be stroppy with a friend who must have spent a pretty penny on that massive flower wreath.

"But aren't you supposed to be dead? The newspaper… the obituary. It said that you were dead."

"I'm alive and kicking!" Mario laughed. "It must have been some sort of mistake. Maybe something to do with their placeholder text. That's what happened to me last year when all those reporters showed up at my door wanting to interview me. It turned out that the newspaper editor hadn't replaced the placeholder name for the recipient of the best actor award in Italians films. Remember how we laughed about that?"

There was a beat of silence at the other end, then Gabriele spoke away from the microphone.

"He's alive! There was a mistake!"

A cheer erupted.

"Where are you? What's going on?" Mario asked.

"We're at your funeral! And you haven't even deigned to turn up. Join us. We've all taken time off for you, so we might as well have a day out together."

Mario rushed to the bakery and bought picnic food, then joined his lifelong friends at the church of San Giuseppe. There, thankfully, nothing was happening: no funeral, no wake, not even a memorial Mass. Because Mario was absolutely alive, and very pleased to be, too.

It turned out that he wasn't half as pleased as his friends were, judging by the hugs, kisses and pats on the back he received. They all set off for a picnic outside town.

On the way, they bought a football to kick around, to remind themselves how good it was to be together, alive and, indeed, kicking.

Grudges were forgotten, dislikes pushed aside, and everyone said thank you to Mario for getting them together, and how clever he'd been to do it without actually kicking the bucket.

"I'm glad you didn't bring your dog. He and I don't get on," Francesco said to Mario once they all sat down for their picnic.

"I know. He bit you once. I'm sorry," Mario replied.

"It's okay," Francesco said, looking a little surprised.

"I love that little dog, but I find it difficult to play with him with my bad back," Mario continued.

"I thought you couldn't be bothered,"

Gabriele admitted, biting into his *panino.*

"Well, a bit of that too."

Antonio cleared his throat. "By the way, Mario, do you still need my electric screwdriver?"

2. A HAIRY SITUATION

It started when his usual barber went on a three-month holiday. Between one thing and another, Sam still hadn't got round to getting a haircut. Now he found himself with an unruly mop of curls that he could hardly run a comb through. Taming his mane was no longer a job for a barber but for a specialised hairdresser.

So Sam searched online for hairdressers specialising in curly hair. He checked reviews and finally made an appointment.

***

"Hi Sam, I'm Hannah and I'll be cutting your hair today," a young woman about his age greeted him.

With blonde locks framing a beautiful face, her name could well have been "angel" as far as Sam was concerned.

"Please, take a seat," she said, showing him to a large swivelling chair in front of a mirror.

Sam sat down obediently. He would have sat on a bed of nails if she'd asked him.

"What can I do for you today?" Hannah asked, sitting on a wheelie stool behind him and making eye contact through the mirror.

"I need a haircut," he said.

"How short?"

Sam's original intention had been to cut his hair short enough to be able to return to his usual barber at the next occasion, but now he wasn't at all keen on the idea. He wanted an excuse to come again soon.

"Just a trim," he replied.

Hannah examined the shape of his last cut, stretched the locks and inspected the split ends.

"I'm sorry my hair is so tangled," he apologised, embarrassed about the state of his hair.

"Don't worry," she said. "It's nothing some conditioner can't solve. Come over to the basins."

As Hannah massaged shampoo into his scalp, he thought that even if he paid with diamonds it wouldn't be enough.

After shampooing his hair and rinsing it, she massaged the conditioner in. Gently and slowly, she ran her brush through his hair, holding it at the roots so as not to hurt him. It was so relaxing that Sam would have fallen asleep had he not been worried about looking stupid in front of Hannah.

Then she wrapped a towel around his head and led him back to the chair in front of the mirror. Now he could watch her as she worked.

"Have you lived here long?" she asked him as she started parting his hair.

Sam wondered whether it was just a standard question to avoid the awkwardness of silence, or if she was genuinely interested in him.

They started a conversation and, as he told her about his life, she also told him about hers.

While her nimble fingers separated, selected and snipped at his hair, Sam wished that it could regrow instantly so that Hannah would have to keep cutting and their time together would never end.

But eventually the next customer arrived, Sam's haircut was finished and it was time for him to leave.

"Would you like another appointment?" Hannah asked.

"Yes, please!" Sam replied with enthusiasm. "When?"

"Twelve weeks… unless your hair grows very fast?"

"At the speed of light."

She hid a smile by looking down at the appointments' screen but he saw her dimples.

"Same day, same time next month?" she asked.

"Yes, please," he agreed.

***

Sam arrived at his appointment early. Hannah welcomed him with her lovely smile and, as she combed and snipped, they talked about their lives, their favourite things and their plans for the future.

It was a pity that the hair salon wasn't a little more private, and as she ran her fingers thought his locks, he wished he could run his through hers too.

But just being near Hannah and talking to her was wonderful.

This time she trimmed even less than the time before, and they fixed the next appointment for the following month.

Sam left the shop with a new bounce to his step as well as to his curls. His hair and his future had never looked better.

***

It was still two weeks, one day and fifteen hours to his next appointment with Hannah when an email arrived in Sam's work inbox.

The company was sponsoring a charity

shave-off in aid of a charity for sick children. Any of the shaved hair that was long enough would be donated to a charity that made wigs for children with cancer.

It was a laudable initiative and Sam had no doubt about sponsoring it. But volunteering to be one of the people who would have their heads shaved? No way. His hair was his link to Hannah. Without any hair on his head, what excuse would he have to see her again?

But as the days went by, colleagues with short hair, long hair and every length in between were signing up to be shaved.

"Sam, your hair would be perfect for a wig," they told him, but Sam shook his head and said no.

He had researched the speed of hair growth. In the best-case scenario, it would take him four months to grow enough hair to justify seeing Hannah again. It was way too long.

He was asked by so many people that he started wearing a beanie hat to hide his hair, stopped going to the canteen for lunch and avoided taking the lift.

But the charity-shave's fever mounted.

Posters of famous people with shaved heads—from Dwayne Johnson to Sinéad O'Connor—appeared on the partitions between the desks. A page was created on the company's intranet for employees to share haircare advice to make sure the hair donated for the wigs was of the best quality. And anyone who owned a set of clippers offered to share them with those who didn't.

The social committee organised drinks and nibbles at the nearby pub for Friday afternoon, straight after the communal shave-off. The idea behind it was that it would be less daunting to venture out into the world without hair for the first time if done in a group.

Critics pointed out that it might be less daunting for the shaved, but not for the passersby who might mistake them for a gang of skinheads.

The charity shave was now the centre of office life. Sam felt so much like a deserter that, the day before the event, he relented and signed up.

***

So many people had signed up for the charity shave that the company gave the entire workforce the afternoon off.

Everyone gathered in the auditorium, and the volunteers went up onto the stage in batches to be shaved.

Sam felt the clippers buzz over his scalp and thought of Hannah. How different this was from her delicate touch. But everyone agreed that his hair would make a beautiful wig, and he was moved to think that his hair would make a sick child happy.

The sponsorship money flocked in, and when it was all collected and counted, Sam topped the charts for the most money raised.

It was a bittersweet achievement, though, because now Sam had to cancel his hair appointment with Hannah.

He was about to ring the salon when it struck him that he could use the cancellation as an excuse to go in person. He pulled his beanie hat down on his head and walked to the salon.

***

Hannah was cutting a client's hair when Sam walked into the shop. As soon as she saw him in the mirror, she turned around and smiled with all her dimples.

"Hello, Sam." She sounded pleased to see him.

"Hello, Hannah."

"How are you?"

"I've come to say that unfortunately I have to cancel my appointment."

Her face fell. "Is everything alright?"

"Sort of." He slowly pulled off his hat.

She gasped. "You've lost all your hair!"

"There was a charity shave at work for children with cancer," he explained.

Her hands flew to her chest. "Phew. I thought you were ill."

Those words fell on Sam's heart like drops of honey coated in courage. Hannah cared about him.

This thought was all he needed to make the step he had wished to make for all these months. It was time to stop hiding behind his hair.

"But we could still see each other, if you like," he suggested. "How about dinner tomorrow?"

All the hairdryers in the room fell silent, and anyone who couldn't see Hannah and Sam through a mirror turned to look at them.

Hannah's cheeks turned pink. "That would be lovely," she said quietly.

But the silence in the room was enough for Sam—and everyone else—to hear it clearly.

3. KEEPING IT COOL

I have only one daughter, and she's the apple of my eye.

She's seven years old but I often feel as if an invisible umbilical cord still connected us. At her every step, the string tugs at me.

Maybe it's because I'm a single mum. So when she takes a tumble in a bouncy castle, my stomach somersaults. During her swimming lesson, I feel like I'm drowning until I see her head poke out of the water. If she's at a sleepover, I spend the night awake.

"You can't keep Izzy wrapped in cotton wool," my mum warns me.

I remind myself that swimming lessons aren't trips on the *Titanic.* Bouncy castle aren't defended by soldiers with vats of boiling oil, and sleepovers aren't dinners with Count

Dracula. So I let Izzy go, hoping that she'll come out unscathed.

But now an ice rink has opened just outside our town. At Izzy's school, it's become everyone's obsession.

"Have you taken Izzy yet?" Shannon, a fellow mum, asks me as we wait for our children at the end of the school day.

"No," I reply. "I'm not sure it's safe."

There's nothing more frightening than children slipping around on metal blades over a sheet of ice.

"Oh, no, it's perfectly safe," she reassures me. "We went there last Sunday and we had a great time."

It's easy for Shannon to be so relaxed. She's seen it all with her five children. I only have Izzy.

"I think we'll pass on the ice rink," I reaffirm.

"You'll be lucky if you can! The children have been talking of nothing else," Shannon tells me.

A moment later, Izzy hurtles out of her classroom, landing right in my arms.

"Guess what?" she asks, her eyes glinting with excitement. "They've opened an ice rink! Everyone has been and they say it was amazing! Can we go?"

"Let's go home first," I reply, hoping that she'll have forgotten about it by the time we arrive.

On the way home, Izzy talks non-stop about the wonders of the ice rink.

"They have these plastic penguins that you can hold on to and push around," she goes on. "When the ice becomes too scratched by all the skates, everyone gets off the rink and they drive this humongous machine to fix it!"

Her excitement was uncontainable.

"Oh, Mum, please, can we go too?"

"Let's talk about it after dinner," I say.

I cook her hot dogs, which are her favourite. I even serve ice cream for pudding. But as soon as she has licked the last drop of ice cream, she starts again.

"Do you think they sell ice cream at the ice rink?"

To distract her, I suggest we watch a movie. She chooses to watch "Frozen".

As Elsa transforms the world around her into an icy wonderland, Izzy watches with huge eyes. "Can we go, please?"

***

As soon as Izzy is safely tucked up in bed, I call my mum.

"I don't know what to do! I've tried distracting her in every way, but she keeps asking to go to the ice rink," I explain.

"Why not? It'll be good fun," Mum remarks.

"I don't think that sharp blades, slippery ice and children are a good mix. I can just see Izzy splayed out on the ice and someone chopping her fingers off with their skates."

The thought sends a shiver down my back.

"I can't imagine that happens often," Mum counters.

"She could fall and knock a tooth out," I say.

"Her teeth are milk teeth and most are wobbly."

I know that I'm running out of arguments. Yet I'm not convinced that the ice rink is safe.

"She's my one and only child," I complain.

"This is her one and only childhood," Mum argues.

I know that she's right.

"I'll take her skating when she turns twelve."

Even if I can't see her, I know that Mum is rolling her eyes.

***

It's the last day of school before the summer holidays and I'm standing in the playground, waiting for Izzy to come out.

If I can only get through today, it will be fine. Once school breaks up, Izzy won't have the other children around her talking about the ice rink and she'll soon forget about it. I cross my fingers behind my back.

One of Shannon's children runs towards her with an envelope in her hand and a huge grin on her face.

"Look, Mummy! I've been invited to Lottie's party!"

"How lovely," Shannon replies with a genuine smile.

A part of me hopes that Izzy has been invited too, because no child likes to feel excluded. But another part dreads the bonanza of junk food, sugar and high spirits that children's parties are.

Izzy arrives, running towards me with an identical envelope.

"Mummy, Lottie's having a birthday party!"

"How nice," I reply with the best smile I can. "Where is it?"

House parties mean bed-jumping competitions, unfenced garden ponds and terrified house pets.

Village halls mean fizzy drinks galore and ear-splitting discos.

Soft play venues mean near-vertical slides and vats of plastic balls laced with snot. They also include foam mazes where stranded children must be rescued with only their cries as a guide to locate them. Every possibility sets me on edge.

Izzy pulls the card out of the envelope and shows it to me proudly. The sparkle in her eyes tells me where the party is even before she confirms it.

"It's at the ice rink!"

My blood freezes.

***

"You'll just have to conquer your fears," Mum advises me.

So here I am, standing on the other side of the puck board. I observe a beaming Izzy struggling to keep upright on her skates.

She's holding on to a plastic penguin and, every few shuffles, she turns her gappy smile at me and waves.

"Keep your hands on the penguin!" I shout, trembling.

Most of her classmates are steadier on their skates than she is. I've only got myself to blame for that. She would be more confident if I had taken her here before.

After a lot of shuffling, near-misses and some confident skating, everyone gets off the rink and heads to the party room for lunch. I can breathe again.

***

I can tell that Izzy is over the moon. Her face is flushed with the exhilaration.

As we troop into a room filled with coloured

balloons, her eyes light up. I quickly understand why when I spot the long table laid out with mini pizzas and hot dogs.

While they eat, Izzy and her friends watch the ice-resurfacing machine through the large window.

It goes up and down, spurting water from its back, making the ice smooth and shiny again. Izzy is enchanted by it.

When it's time to return to the rink for another skating session, her hot dog is still only half-finished. She's eaten all the bread first, the way she always does, leaving the sausage last because it's the best part.

She gets up to hurry out onto the ice with the others, but I call out.

"Izzy, finish your food before you go skating, please."

I see the ghost of a concerned frown flit across her face as she grabs hold of the sausage and a ketchup packet.

"Thank you, sweetheart," I say distractedly.

My eye is drawn back out onto the ice. The other children are filing through the gap in the barrier. The rink is even smoother and shinier than before and I feel my chest tightening. The fresh ice is bright in the fluorescent lighting. I can't help but imagine it has a menacing glint to it.

"Okay, Mummy, I'm done!" Izzy tells me.

My attention is drawn back to my daughter.

She waves her empty paper plate at me to show that the hot dog is gone.

Before I can say anything more, she dashes away to put her skates on.

Her hot dog dilemma has made Izzy the last to enter the rink and all the penguins are taken. My heart is in my mouth as I see her step out onto the ice rink, gripping the sides.

She starts skating without support, tentatively at first, then more confidently.

She's doing it! She's skating all on her own!

I'm terrified, but a little proud too.

"Mummy, look at me!" she shouts, turning towards the viewers' seating area.

But as she turns her head, her feet turn too, and the rest of her body follows. A pirouette? No, not a pirouette. My little girl is falling!

I hear a thud as she loses control of her legs. She topples onto the ice, belly down, sprawled like Bambi on the frozen lake.

Time seems to slow down. It's like something from my worst fears. What looks like a severed finger, splattered with blood, rolls out across the ice. A scream pierces the air, but it's not Izzy's. It's mine. Everything goes dark.

***

"She's fainted," I hear through the woolly fog in my head.

"Kelly? Are you alright?" It's Shannon's voice.

I open my eyes slowly to a circle of other mums' heads, all looking down at me with concern. I'm lying down across several seats.

"Where's Izzy?" I mumble.

Izzy's head peeks out through the little crowd.

"Mummy, are you okay?"

I remember the finger on the ice. Panic heaves through my stomach. I spring up to sitting.

"Show me your hands."

With a puzzled look, Izzy offers her hands for inspection.

Nothing seems amiss. I count her fingers all the same. Every one of them is where it should be.

"I saw your finger cut off on the ice!" I protest.

Izzy looks embarrassed. "That was my hot dog," she explains.

In a split second my horror is displaced by confusion.

"Your..." My mind is racing. "Izzy, what do you mean it was your hot dog?"

Izzy turns a little pink. "I wanted to skate

but I wanted to save the sausage for later," she admits. "It's the best bit."

I shake my head.

"Are you alright?" I double check.

"Only if I can I have another hot dog when I finish skating."

I nod, still feeling a little shell-shocked.

She glances at the rink where her friends are still skating. The staff are sweeping the hot dog off the ice.

"Can I go back to skating now?" she asks.

It hits me that, most of the times when I worry for her, she's absolutely fine. The only one who isn't fine is me.

"Off you go," I tell her with a smile.

***

Over the summer holidays, I take Izzy to the ice rink a few times. I even have a go myself.

When she asks if she can have a birthday party there, I don't shoot it down.

"I think we can do that, with precautions."

I'm thinking sturdy gloves, helmets and gum shields on request.

"Thank you!" she squeals. "Can I invite the whole class?"

"Yes, you can. For the snack, how about some nice carrot sticks, slices of fruit and banana chips?" I suggest hopefully.

But Izzy twists her mouth. "Can't we have hot

dogs instead?"

4. OLD BIKE, NEW TRICKS

Rob enjoyed his Saturday rides with his cycling club. He relished exercise, time outdoors and friendship, and he got all these in spades every weekend, riding with the club.

There was only one cloud in this otherwise clear sky. His bike.

The other members of the club had ultra-light, state-of-the-art racing bicycles. Rob's one was a heavy, old road bike.

The only times when he was glad about his bike was in the middle of a ride, when he and his fellow club members would stop at a café. Then, Rob was the only one who could enjoy his coffee without worrying about theft. No thief in his right mind would steal his cheap bike when it was parked next to much more expensive ones.

But all the rest of the times, Rob struggled to keep up with the group on his heavy bike.

He felt his disadvantage more keenly whenever hills were involved. While the others raced up ahead on their super-light carbon machines, he struggled up on the slopes like a tortoise. Going downhill, his bike's lack of disc brakes meant that he didn't dare go as fast as the others.

Sometimes, on his weekdays solo rides, other cyclists he met on the road looked down on his bike and didn't greet him, as if he weren't a real cyclist like them.

That weekend, the famous Tour of Britain cycling race was due to pass through Rob's village. The club had organised to ride up the hill, stop at a suitable viewing spot and watch the world's best cyclists make the toughest local hill look easy.

Rob wasn't looking forward to turning up in his amateurish bike to an event where the world's "who's who" of the best bicycles would be on display. But he was keen on seeing the race and being with his friends, so he swallowed his pride and joined the party.

***

Every local cycling club had flocked to watch the race, and they had come in their best bicycles and their branded gear. Once again, Rob was ashamed of his bicycle.

Then, suddenly, cow bells sounded, the race

supervisor's car rushed past, hooting, and everyone knew that the first cyclists were approaching.

Word rippled through the crowd that Marcus Flyingfish was on the lead. Having broken away from the main peloton, the British champion was belting up the hill as if the road were on fire. The crowd cheered, everyone wanting the veteran cyclist to win his last race before retirement.

But suddenly, his bicycle chain snapped. Marcus's foot slipped. The crowd gasped. Marcus wobbled to a halt and glanced apprehensively over his shoulder. He needed a spare bicycle but the service cars with the spare bikes on the roof were nowhere to be seen.

"The service cars are stuck behind the peloton, further down the hill," a cameraman on the back of a motorbike told the champion.

Rob realised that, if Marcus waited for the service car, he would be overtaken by the other cyclists and lose any hope of victory. It would be a real pity as he wasn't far from the finish line.

There were many good bikes among the amateur cyclists in the crowd, but nobody offered theirs. Rob hadn't even considered offering his cheap, heavy bike. But seeing the champion in such dire need, he rushed out onto the road and handed it to him.

The champion's face lit up, he thanked Rob and raced the rest of the way up the hill.

Rob watched his bike climb the hill faster than it ever had before. He would never blame his slowness on his bike again! He also might never see his bike again: Marcus didn't even know his name.

***

Marcus Flyingfish won that race thanks to Rob's bike. When he was interviewed on TV, he said that he owed his victory to the generous bystander who had lent him his bike. TV footage of Rob walking out onto the road and offering his bike to the stranded champion were all over the coverage on TV and newspapers.

When Rob approached the team to recover his bike, he was personally welcomed by Marcus, and was gifted a state-of-the-art bicycle in the team's colours. Rob was now a legend not just in his cycling club or in his village, but all over the cycling world, and so was his old bicycle. Although the new one was a lot lighter, faster and beautiful, he preferred to ride his old one. And when other cyclists met him on the roads, even if they didn't recognise him, they always recognised his old bike and gave him a thumbs up.

5. PASS THE PARCEL

"Delivered? But I haven't received anything," Julie said to the man at the other end of the phone.

She had called the shop only to check why her parcel was late. She certainly hadn't expected to hear that it had been delivered.

"It was left behind your side gate."

"But I don't have a side gate."

"Your neighbour's gate, perhaps?"

Did her neighbour have a side gate? She didn't remember: she had only just moved in.

"Look, I paid extra for an earlier delivery. I need my parcel urgently."

"I can email you the photo the driver has taken on delivery, if that helps?" the man suggested.

"Yes, please."

With luck she would recognise one of her neighbours' gates and could knock on their door and retrieve her parcel.

But when the email came through, she didn't recognise the wooden gate. With the email on her phone, she went out into the street, checking her neighbours' gates.

No: the gate in the photo didn't belong to either of her next-door neighbours, nor the houses opposite. She examined the photo again, looking for clues.

Nothing.

It was too close up to show any house number or other useful details. All she could do was try to put herself in the shoes of the delivery person and guess what they might have done.

She lived at number eight and, on a couple of occasions, the postman had put the mail for number 18 through her letterbox. Could the delivery person have made the same mistake, but the other way round? Julie headed off towards number 18.

Reassuringly, number 18 had a wooden side gate just like the one in the photo. She smiled to herself and knocked on the door.

A young woman about her age opened the door with a friendly smile. Julie told her about her parcel.

"Nice to meet you at last," the woman said. "I sometimes get your post, but not this time.

I usually slip it through your letterbox when I get home from work."

"So it's you! I thought our postman was doing extra shifts when I received letters in the evenings. I'm Julie." Julie offered her hand.

"I'm Jemima. That might explain why the postman gets us mixed up!" Jemima chuckled and Julie instantly felt a connection.

She discovered that Jemima had moved in recently too, and she worked in the offices next to Julie's place of work.

"Maybe we should exchange numbers. We could have a cup of coffee some day?" Jemima suggested.

"Sure." One day. When Julie eventually got her parcel. "I'd better get going and carry on looking for my parcel," Julie said after they'd swapped numbers. Before she got too weak, grumpy or headachy.

A little further down the street, she spotted another wooden gate. This time, a butterflies-in-the-stomach-handsome man answered the door.

"I'm sorry, I haven't received anything." He scratched the back of his neck pensively. "At least, I don't think I have. Let me check behind the gate."

He had only just stepped out of the house when the most adorable puppy zipped out the front door and almost bumped against his master's ankle.

"No, George. Stay," the man instructed him.

The puppy ran circles around him. He wasn't going to be left behind.

"I'll hold him, if you like," Julie offered.

"Yes, please. He doesn't like to be left alone in the house," the man said.

He picked up the puppy and handed him to her. Their fingers brushed and a rush of electricity ran up Julie's arm, threatening to melt the few remaining neurons that hadn't already been liquefied by the man's magnetic blue gaze and the puppy's big brown eyes.

George was soft, warm and smelled of… biscuits? The man must have been baking, because that same delicious smell was wafting out the front door. Julie imagined sitting inside, in front of a plate of biscuits and a cup of coffee.

"No parcels," the man said.

He made to take George back from her, but the puppy held on to her jumper with his claws.

"He really likes you," the man said.

"He's adorable. If you ever need someone to look after him when you're out, I'd be happy to help."

"That would be great. Tonight I was going to buy biscuits for my students tomorrow, but

I didn't want to leave George alone so I had to bake some instead."

"I've been enjoying the heavenly smell." Julie smiled.

"Would you like to come in and have some?"

Julie was tempted, but what about her parcel?

"That's very kind of you, thanks, but I'd better be on my way and carry on looking for my parcel."

"You can come back when you've found it, if you like. My name is Jack." He scribbled on a piece of paper. "Here is my number, in case you need anything."

"Thank you. I'm Julie." She dialled his number on her phone and rang it. "Now you have my number too."

Julie walked away from Jack's place feeling a little lightheaded. It was either the effect of meeting her gorgeous neighbour or of missing her parcel. Thankfully, not much farther down the road there was another wooden gate.

Julie rang the doorbell and children started screaming inside. Oh, dear, she shouldn't have disturbed these people. Too late now.

The door opened and a harassed-looking woman stood on the threshold with a screaming child on one hip and a toddler pulling at her dress on the other side.

"I'm really sorry to disturb you."

"It's okay," the woman answered good-naturedly.

Julie quickly explained about her missing parcel. As soon as she showed them the photos of the parcel, the child quietened, which Julie was very grateful about, as she was starting to develop a headache.

"I'm sorry, but we haven't received anything," the woman said.

"Would you like a cup of tea?" the small child asked, letting go of her mother's dress. She spoke in exactly the same tone as her mother, which made Julie smile.

"Thank you, but I have to look for my parcel."

Not only did she need to get her parcel before the headache got its grip on her, but surely hosting a tea party for a stranger was the last thing the child's mother wanted.

"How about another time?" the woman said, to Julie's surprise.

"Sure," Julie replied.

The woman seemed very nice, and if she could make time for it, so could Julie.

"Yes, yes!" the children shouted.

"I'm Miranda, and these are Stacey and Chris."

"Lovely to meet you. I'm Julie."

They exchanged numbers and the children waved at her until she was out of sight.

Now Julie had exhausted all the wooden gates in her street. Her parcel could be anywhere: a wrong digit in her postcode could have sent it to another town. How would she ever find it? All she could do was explain the situation to the seller, ask for a replacement and wait another week.

She trudged home feeling heavy, tired and headachy.

She had just started composing the email when the doorbell rang. She traipsed to the door and opened it.

A dapper elderly gentleman stood before her, holding a parcel identical to the one in the photo.

"I believe this is for you," he said.

"My parcel! Thank you so much!"

Julie all but snatched the box from the man's hands.

"I live at number eight, but in Magnolia Street. The delivery guy must have turned too early," the man surmised.

Magnolia Street was two streets away, which meant that this man had gone out of his way to deliver the heavy parcel to her.

"I'm really sorry about the trouble," Julie

apologised.

"It's not your fault."

But neither was it his. How could she thank him?

"Have you got time?" she asked him.

He smiled. "Plenty."

"How about a cup of coffee or tea?" she suggested. "I'm Julie."

"And I'm David. Please to meet you." He glanced at the parcel. Printed on the box was a picture of its contents. "I'd love a cup of coffee."

"Great. Come in," Julie told him. "Excuse the cardboard boxes everywhere. I've just moved in."

"So have I," he replied.

Then Julie had an idea. "Would you like to meet some of the people in this neighbourhood?"

His face lit up. "I'd love to."

"Then I'll make a few phone calls. I know some people who might like to come for coffee too."

People who might bring over an adorable puppy, two friendly children and some freshly baked biscuits, she thought.

"Great," the man replied. "And if you like, while you make the calls, I'll take your new coffee machine out of the box..."

6. BUCK THE TREND

Alessandra glanced at her watch again. If she managed to leave the supermarket in the next five minutes, she could beat the Naple's rush-hour traffic and pick up Francesca from ballet and Mario from football on time.

But there was still another customer before her in the queue for the till. Maybe she shouldn't have tried to squeeze in a supermarket visit, but this week Francesca was preparing for a ballet performance and she was on a very specific diet which required fresh ricotta for supper.

Alessandra had almost reached the belt when a woman came in from the side and put her shopping basket down on the belt ahead of her.

"There's a queue," Alessandra said politely to the woman.

"I was after this lady," the woman argued,

pointing to the customer in front, who was just paying. "I just went back to get some milk."

"But you didn't even leave your basket behind," Alessandra pointed out.

"You can ask her," the woman returned, pointing to the lady in front, who shrugged in response. "I'm in a hurry," the queue-jumper added, given that nobody around them seemed willing to support her claim.

"So am I, and so is everyone else!" Alessandra exclaimed, struggling to keep calm.

The queue-jumper turned her back on her and started unloading the contents of her basket onto the belt.

Alessandra couldn't believe the woman's impudence. Surely the cashier wouldn't serve her, she thought. But the man started scanning the woman's groceries.

At that, Alessandra saw red. She slammed her bag of ricotta onto the belt with such force that the bag broke, sending fresh sheep ricotta splattering onto the side of the till, the cashier, the other woman and Alessandra.

"Mind what you're doing!" the queue-jumper snapped.

Alessandra shrieked with frustration, threw her basket on the floor and ran out of the supermarket.

There was no parking near the ballet school,

and Alessandra had to double park next to another car.

Francesca's class was running late, so she needn't have stressed herself at the supermarket after all. What had got into her? Splattering everyone with ricotta and storming out of the shop was unlike her. Now she had no supper for the family and there was no way she could show her face in that supermarket ever again.

Someone hooted from the car she had blocked in.

"Calm down!" she shouted, turning on her engine to move the car.

Her jaw tightened and her pulse rose again. Maybe she was the one who needed to calm down.

***

Ornella admired her work on her tablet. It had taken painstaking research to construct the family tree.

Her ancestors were such a motley crew—dukes and swindlers, doctors and criminals, sailors and mayors—that she wouldn't have believed it if she hadn't seen the marriage and birth entries with her very own eyes.

Her great-great-great grandfather had managed to come out of the Bourbon king's dungeons alive and had gone on to amass a fortune trading spices with the English.

His son had skilfully used that money to buy the land and title of an impoverished duke and, for a short while, the family had enjoyed wealth and status. But his sons had gambled everything away.

"Hello, Mum," a voice said from the flat's entrance.

"Alessandra, what a lovely surprise!"

But Ornella's happiness drained away as soon as she saw her daughter's face. Alessandra looked frazzled and upset.

"Are you all right, my dear?"

"I'm not having a good day. It's a long story."

"I'd be happy to hear it."

"Sorry, but I'm in a rush. Can you lend me a bottle of tomato sauce and some salad? I haven't got anything for supper."

"Bring everyone here for supper," Ornella suggested.

"I'd love to," her daughter replied, "but I've things to do at home."

Ornella didn't insist but gave her some tomato sauce she had made that morning, along with some fresh fruit and veggies. Then she accompanied Alessandra to the door and waved her off.

***

As soon as Alessandra got home, Mario gave her his football kit to be washed because he needed it again the next day.

While the pasta was on the hob, Alessandra loaded the washing machine. With luck, it would be finished and ready to be hung out to dry before she went to bed.

When her husband and kids had been fed and had rushed off to do their work in their rooms, she finally sat down to eat.

Her mother's tomato sauce was deliciously sweet and tangy, just like the feelings swirling in her chest: the sweetness of her mother's love that she could taste through the sauce, and the tangy sourness of having had to say goodbye too soon.

That afternoon, she had seen in her mother's eyes the same longing for togetherness that she had felt in her own heart. She would have loved to stay, sit on the sofa next to her mum and tell her about her day.

Tomorrow, if her children didn't need her too much, she would try to find some time to visit her mum.

***

Ornella had been thinking about her daughter all day but hadn't wanted to disturb her. So when Alessandra turned up that afternoon, Ornella was overjoyed.

Alessandra sank wearily into the sofa.

"Would you like a cup of coffee?" Ornella offered.

"I'd love one, but I can't stay. I need to collect Francesca's tutu from the seamstress. What's this?" Alessandra was glancing at the family tree on Ornella's tablet.

"I've been doing some research on our family's ancestry."

Alessandra studied the family tree.

"Goodness, we are descended from a duke! I'd love to hear all the things that you've found out," Alessandra added. "What a pity I have to go so soon."

"Could Francesca pick up her own tutu?" Ornella asked. "She's sixteen after all."

"She would make a mess of it. For last year's show she almost came home with her friend's tutu if I hadn't been there to remind her to check the name on the parcel."

"If she gets the wrong tutu, she will learn to pay more attention next time, don't you think?"

Alessandra smiled, as if Ornella's comment were a joke. But Ornella was serious. How could Francesca grow up if Alessandra did everything for her? How could she learn from her mistakes if she was never allowed to make any?

"Then, after the seamstress, I have to dash to the stadium to collect Mario from football practice," her daughter continued.

"Couldn't he take a bus?"

"It would take him more than an hour to get home, while it's only ten minutes by car."

"But he is eighteen," Ornella pointed out. "If you keep ferrying him around, he'll never have any incentive to study for his driving licence."

Her daughter's face clouded.

Oh, dear. She was playing the part of the interfering and overbearing grandma.

"Bringing up children today isn't the same as when you were young," Alessandra said curtly. "I have to go now. Can I take a photo of our family tree? I'll look at it better when I have time."

"Of course."

But when did her daughter imagine that she would have time?

***

Mario's football practice was running late. Another mother, sitting on the bleachers next to Alessandra, was doing an online grocery shop on her phone.

A father further down the row was having a loud work phone call, while a teacher was marking homework, balancing it on her knees.

Her fellow parents were snatching bits of time around their children's many engagements. Alessandra didn't remember her mother doing anything like that when she was little.

She chased the thought away and whipped out her phone. She might as well start shopping for groceries online herself, given that she had burnt her bridges at the supermarket next to her flat.

But as her phone lit up, the photo of her family tree appeared. She was immediately absorbed and couldn't take her eyes off it. She studied it carefully and a pattern started to emerge. Peasant, merchant, duke, beggar. Cabin boy, second officer, captain, convict.

It reminded her of an English saying: "Clogs to clogs in three generations." Judging by her family tree, it was true!

Her mother had made notes on the side. The merchant had purchased title and land from an impoverished duke, but his children had gambled it away and ended up begging in the streets. When the family's fortunes had risen again, the ship captain's son had succumbed to drinking and landed in the king's prison.

What was it about wealth and comforts that seemed to slip so easily out of people's hands?

She counted from the last fall in family fortune to her generation. It seemed that the return to poverty was long overdue. Suddenly she remembered her mother's words. "If you keep ferrying him around, he'll never have any incentive to study for his driving licence."

It was true. By taking away hardships and difficulties from her children's lives, she was stopping them from developing the ingenuity, enterprise and drive that come from need. By giving them everything they wanted, she was setting them on a path towards destruction. How could she not have realised it before? She had loved her children wrongly.

Instead of doing a grocery shop online, she rang her daughter.

"Hello, darling. I need you to go to the supermarket downstairs and buy something for our supper."

***

Ornella had just finished adding another layer to the family tree when the door of her flat clicked open.

"Hello, Mum."

It was Alessandra.

Ornella's heart leapt with happiness. She had been thinking of her daughter since their little disagreement.

"Can I stay for a cup of coffee?" Alessandra asked.

"I'd love you to. Have you got time?"

"Yes. The kids will ring me when supper is ready."

Ornella wasn't sure she had heard correctly. "The kids are cooking supper?"

"Yes, and they're doing a lot of other things that I used to do for them. I looked at our family tree and realised that a beggar and a convict are long overdue, and I don't want it to be my children. You were right, Mum," she admitted. "I was mollycoddling them. So far they've enjoyed the challenges I've thrown at them and seem to be thriving."

"I'm so pleased for you!"

"And the best part is that I don't have to go to the supermarket anymore."

"I'm not sure I'm following you, but I guess that it's a long story."

"It is." Alessandra smiled. "But at least now I have the time to tell you."

7. THE IDEAL BOYFRIEND

Josh had fallen in love with Ella. Together with other students, they shared a flat in the university's halls, but their different timetables meant that they only met at dinnertime.

Josh spent hours in the kitchen, engaged in lengthy and complicated recipes, preferably involving the tossing of food in the air. He would time his recipes to coincide with her dinner so that he could sit at the kitchen table with her.

If their flatmates had worked out that he was holding a candle—or rather, a flame—for her, they hadn't said anything. And if Ella had any inkling about his feelings for her, she hadn't shown it either.

With every day that passed, the thought that some other guy, braver than himself, would beat him to the post gave Josh considerable anxiety.

So one morning, Josh gathered his courage and walked to her room with the intention of asking her out.

The door was open. He knocked but nobody answered. He peered inside. Nobody there.

Something attracted Josh's attention—an A4 sheet of paper, pinned to a corkboard, covered in pink hearts.

Josh's own heart sank to the pit of his stomach. Was there already someone in Ella's heart?

He took a step in. On the sheet, there was a list. Josh read:

1. *Intelligent*
2. *Loyal*
3. *Good company*
4. *Affectionate*
5. *Not too sleepy*
6. *Not too loud*
7. *Not too energetic*
8. *Not aggressive*
9. *Loves people and children*

Josh couldn't believe his luck. This had to be Ella's wish list for the ideal boyfriend, and it could only mean that she didn't already have a love interest.

Armed with this list, he could make sure to tick all her boxes.

He wasn't sure how intelligent Ella wanted her man, but he was loyal and affectionate with the people he loved. He could be good company when he was in the mood, and he could be quiet when needed. He loved people and he loved children, so that wasn't a problem at all. And he didn't have an aggressive bone in his body.

He just had to show Ella that he ticked all her boxes.

But before he had read down to the bottom of the list, he heard steps in the corridor. It wouldn't look good if Ella found him snooping in her room.

He squeezed out of there and back to his room. Next stop would be the library.

***

Intelligent, loyal

Ella thought of Josh while she was dissecting a fish in her afternoon zoology class.

The night before, Josh had cooked a whole sea bass with ginger and spices and had shared it with her, but only after cleaning it of its bones.

Josh was caring and sweet like this, and she had fallen for him from the first week. But dating a flatmate was a taboo in the students' community. If the relationship broke down, there would be tension in the flat and everyone would suffer.

But this didn't mean that she couldn't enjoy watching his cooking displays—pancake-tossing, ultra-fast slicing, blow-torch antics—and having dinner with him.

She just had to keep it strictly within the friendship and give no hints of her true feelings.

Walking home, she wondered what he might be cooking tonight.

But when she got to the kitchen, Josh wasn't cooking anything at all. Instead, he sat at the kitchen table with his nose in a book, frowning in concentration, and a sandwich in his hand.

"Only a sandwich for dinner?" she asked him, surprised.

"No time to cook. I'm busy reading this," he said, flipping over the cover of the book.

The title read "Advanced Quantum Physics."

"But I thought you studied Art," she said, confused.

"This isn't for my course. I just like to stretch my mind," he said, before returning his attention to the pages of the tome.

Ella microwaved a potato for her dinner and sat next to him, waiting for the moment he would put the book down and chat with her as usual. But she finished her potato, her baked beans and her apple, and that moment didn't come.

This wasn't the dinner together she had been looking forward to all day. She wracked her brains for topics that could interest him enough to put the book down.

"Which is your favourite football team?" she asked.

He looked up at her with apprehension, as if the question were a test.

"Er…" he hesitated. "Manchester United?"

"You don't seem convinced," she said.

"Oh, no, I am! The most loyal fan!" he hurried to say.

"It's fine, I don't mind which team you support. I'm not into football," she reassured him.

"But if you were," he went on, "and you tried to make me change my mind about which team I support, I would never. Loyalty is very important to me, and I have it in spades!"

Ella was confused. Josh was behaving very strangely tonight.

He returned to his book and Ella's hope of spending a cosy evening chatting with him evaporated.

***

Good company, affectionate

Josh was trying to get his head around the

extra dimensions of string theory, when a thought came into his mind. He needed to consider all the items in Ella's list at once.

What good was it to tick the intelligence box by reading this tome at the dinner table if he then failed the "good company" requisite?

He slammed the book closed and, turning to Ella, asked her how her day had been.

She instantly smiled and told him about the fish dissection that had gone wrong and the experiment that hadn't worked.

He wanted to squeeze her hand in sympathy, but with the kitchen full of people, it didn't feel like the right place to be intimate and affectionate like that.

They needed to go out somewhere they wouldn't be surrounded by people who knew them.

"Shall we go for a walk?" he suggested.

She hesitated and he immediately regretted offering such a lame suggestion.

He needed to take Ella somewhere quiet so that he could be affectionate, but he also needed to be good company and entertaining. He must show her that he could be the life of the party.

Of course, what he needed was a party!

"Let's go to the nightclub!"

***

Not too energetic

Ella regretted telling Josh about her day's misadventures. Of course she had bored him with her moaning!

But to have bored him so much that he now needed a night out at the nightclub was a little crushing. Also because she would have rather continued chatting with him in the kitchen.

She had almost turned down his invitation but then thought better of it—what if he went out without her anyway?

She hated thinking of him dancing with other girls.

So now she was on the dance floor, bobbing half-heartedly to the music while her feet were killing her.

On the contrary, Josh was dancing like a dervish. He gestured to follow him to the stage. That was where the most extroverted dancers showed off their moves. Certainly not for her.

"No, thanks," she shouted over the loud music. "I'm not feeling as energetic as you."

As if she had pressed a switch, he stilled suddenly. Had she said something wrong?

Taking her hand, he led her away from the dance floor towards the sofas. How considerate of him!

They sat down and her feet thanked her. But she started to feel guilty about taking him away from the dance floor, which he had seemed to enjoy very much.

"You don't have to sit with me, if you want to dance," she offered.

"Oh, I'm totally out of energy. I'm not an energetic guy," he said, while his foot betrayed him, tapping to the rhythm.

Ella was ever more confused.

***

Not aggressive

Josh told himself that he must be more careful. He had almost failed the "not too energetic" requirement. Thankfully, he had stopped himself just in time.

Now that they were sitting in a quiet corner with the music in the background and soft lighting, it must be his chance to tick off the "affectionate" box.

But what exactly would she like him to do? The same gesture could be considered restrained by someone and too forward by someone else. This was a territory fraught with danger.

So Josh did what he had wanted to do when they were in the kitchen and she was offloading about her bad day—he patted her hand.

"You can go and dance, if you want," she said, misunderstanding the gesture. "I'll just have a little more rest, then I'll join you."

Josh regretted suggesting going to the nightclub when she had already told him how tiring her day had been.

"No, it's fine. We can sit here as long as you like," Josh said.

"Thanks," she said with obvious relief.

"And if you'd like to go home, that's fine too," he said.

"Actually, I do. Do you mind?"

"Not at all!"

Outside, the night was quiet and the air refreshing, and the moon had risen in a clear sky. It was a nicely romantic setting for ticking the affectionate box.

Josh was about to reach for Ella's hand when he heard some shouting.

"My phone! Give it back! Thief!"

He whipped round and saw a girl chasing after a guy who was clutching a glittery pink phone, running in his direction.

Josh didn't think twice. He intercepted the thief and tackled him to the ground. The man punched and tried to wriggle free but Josh pinned him down. A scuffle ensued until the girl caught up, snatched her phone from the thief and Josh let the guy go.

The girl thanked him profusely, but now Josh had a bleeding lip and a black eye, and Ella looked shaken.

Josh remembered point six of the boyfriend's wish list—"not aggressive"—and groaned. There was no way he hadn't failed that one.

***

Not too sleepy, not too loud

Despite the long night out, Josh had set his alarm at six o'clock so that he could tick the "not too sleepy" box in Ella's list.

It had taken a very loud alarm, positioned far from the bed, and all Josh's willpower, to drag him out of bed at that hour.

And now he was groggily preparing his breakfast in the kitchen.

Ella appeared at the door.

"You're up early," she said, rubbing her eyes.

"I don't need much sleep. I'm not a sleepy person," he said, immediately betrayed by a yawn.

"I thought you liked sleeping in," she said, looking confused.

"People can grow out of bad habits," he said. "You're up early too. Early lecture?"

"I was woken up by your alarm. I could hear it through the wall," she said.

Oh, no. This was going to make him fail the "not too loud" point.

"I'm so sorry. You won't hear a noise

coming from my room again!" he promised.

He rushed to the shops and bought a pair of wireless headphones which he connected to his TV, laptop, phone and even his alarm clock.

***

Ella was ever more puzzled by Josh's behaviour. He seemed to be a different person, and she wasn't sure she liked the new Josh as much as the old one. Tonight, at dinnertime, she would try and find out what had happened.

When she got home that evening, she headed for the kitchen, hoping to find him there, singing as he cooked, as usual. But he wasn't there.

She knocked on his door, but there was no answer. All was silent inside, but light seeped under the door. Was he ignoring her?

He must be cross with her about last night. If she had snatched the phone from the thief while Josh was tackling him, perhaps he would have received fewer punches. Instead, she had stood on the spot, petrified with fear for him, until the girl had caught up.

She knocked once more. No answer again. So she padded over to the kitchen sadly, resigned to have dinner on her own.

***

Loves people and children

Josh pulled his headphones off. He had

been wearing them all afternoon and now his ears were sweaty, but after waking Ella with his alarm, he couldn't risk breaking her list's decibel requirement again.

Was she still upset with him for waking her up? He was about to find out.

He stepped out of his room to go to the kitchen, when two children ran out of another room, cutting in front of him.

"Sorry," Daisy, another of his flatmates, said. "My nieces have been cooped up in my room all day and they're bouncing off the walls! My sister has left them with me for the day and they're driving me crazy."

Josh's ears pricked up. Wasn't "loves people and children" one of the items on the list?

"If you like, I'll help you entertain them," he offered.

"Oh, yes, please!" Daisy agreed.

"I'll fetch my football and I'll meet you out on the grass," he told Daisy.

The patch of grass at the entrance of their block was in good view of the kitchen window. With luck, Ella would see him entertain the children and he would have ticked the "love children" box.

***

Ella had finished her supper but there was still no sign of Josh in the kitchen.

It saddened her that he'd rather eat in his room and give up on a cooked supper than risk meeting her in the kitchen.

Could he be unwell instead?

She was about to head back to his room when she heard a voice coming from outside.

"Pass it here!"

She could recognise that voice in a million.

Ella ran to the window and her heart squeezed when she saw him kicking a ball with Daisy and two little girls.

So this was the reason for all his strange behaviours—he was in love with Daisy!

***

After playing football, Josh had given piggyback rides to Daisy's nieces and played aeroplanes with them, followed by hide-and-seek and tag. By the time the girls' mum had come to collect them, he was exhausted.

He had hoped that Ella would come out and join them, or at least watch them from the kitchen window, but there had been no sign of her all evening.

He met her the next morning in the kitchen, when she was having breakfast. He had taken to waking up early. The day became so much longer.

"Hi, how are you?" he asked her jovially.

"Fine. You?" she replied without a smile.

Was she cross with him? He couldn't have woken her up again—his alarm now went through his headphones.

"Did you have fun playing with Daisy's nieces last night?" she asked, avoiding eye contact.

This was his chance to impress her.

"Oh, yes! They're great kids. I love children."

"But Daisy is your flatmate," she went on. "Flatmates shouldn't date, everyone knows that—don't you?"

"I'm not dating Daisy!"

"But you want to, don't you?"

"Not at all! You've totally misunderstood."

Was this why she was giving him the cold shoulder? Was she jealous?

Emboldened by that thought, he gathered his courage.

"I played with her nieces because they were bored, and because I wanted to impress you. I would like us to be more than friends," he confessed.

"Oh." A smile spread across Ella's face. She looked beautiful. "Actually, I'd like that too," she admitted shyly. "I just thought it wouldn't be a good idea, as we are flatmates."

"But in a few months, we'll move out of here and we won't be flatmates anymore," Josh said. "We just have to make sure we don't break up before then. I'll do my best to tick all your boxes so you don't have to break up with me."

She looked a little puzzled, then smiled and kissed him.

***

That evening, on his way to the kitchen, Josh knocked on Ella's door.

"Would you like to have supper together?" he asked her.

"I'd love to. We could also cook together."

"Excellent idea."

But Josh's happiness drained away as his gaze fell on the corkboard. The list with the pink hearts was still there. Why would she need the wish list if she already had a boyfriend?

Then his gaze fell on the last item in the list, the one he hadn't managed to read the first time. *Gets along with other dogs*, it said.

Josh burst into laughter.

All this time, he had tried to tick all the boxes of Ella's wish list for a pet dog!

8. A MOTHER'S WORK

Mario Rachel put down the Winnie-The-Pooh hairbrush. Why did brushing her daughter's hair take so much longer than combing her own?

"Done. Go and put your shoes on, sweetie."

"Can you make plaits?" Charlotte asked, puppy-eyed.

Rachel glanced at her phone. It was already 7.45am, the time when she'd hoped to be in her classroom, setting up her Year 10 Chemistry lesson.

"Sorry darling, we're running late."

"Running" being the key word. These days she was always running, always struggling to catch up.

"James, put your shoes on!"

"I can't. I've had a little accident."

"Little accident" were two words that never failed to give Rachel goosebumps.

James stood by the kitchen table with an exploded pouch of fruit juice in his hands dripping purple liquid over his trousers, his socks and the floor.

"It burst."

"Not by itself," Rachel said, but there was no time. "Change your trousers and socks," she instructed as she wiped the floor.

"Can I have a packed lunch too?" Charlotte asked, getting in Rachel's way.

"It's fish fingers today. You love them."

"I don't anymore," Charlotte said.

"They're not actually made of fishes' fingers. We've discussed this before."

"I know that, because fish don't have fingers. Also because they're actually made of birds' eyes," Charlotte replied.

"No baby, that's just the name of the brand." Rachel shot a stern glance at her son who looked away guiltily. Never again would she ask him to help his sister choose her lunches on the school menu.

When everyone had piled into the car, it felt like a small miracle. And Rachel finally drove off.

***

Claire watched her neighbour, Rachel, get into the car with James and Charlotte.

Claire missed the time when her own

children were that age, when she was still brushing little girls' hair, tying shoelaces, preparing packed lunches. These days, the only lunches she packed were for her husband.

"Sorry, I forgot to tell you," Steve said. "We're having a lunchtime meeting and the company is providing sandwiches."

"Is this about the takeover?"

Steve winced a little. Claire knew that he feared for his job.

"Yes. I might be late home tonight. Will you be alright?"

Shouldn't she be asking him that? But since the children had left home, everyone seemed concerned about her.

"Of course."

They kissed goodbye and she watched him drive off.

All their neighbours' drives were now empty—everyone was at work—and a wave of loneliness swept over her.

Maybe she should get a job too. It would relieve some of the financial worry and give her something to do. But the only job she'd ever loved was being a mum.

Just then, her neighbour reappeared. Why were James and Charlotte still in the car?

***

Rachel rested her head on the steering wheel

and let tears trickle down her cheeks. Why did the burst pipe have to happen in her children's school, not hers?

She'd have to call work to say she couldn't come in—again. Last week it was James's flu. Now this. Every time, she let everyone down.

***

When she saw Charlotte trip on the doorstep and take a tumble, Claire shot out of her door.

"It's fine. You haven't even grazed the skin," she comforted the bawling girl.

But when her mother emerged from the car, it was clear that Rachel was the one who needed comforting.

Minutes later everyone was in Claire's kitchen with tea and hot chocolate. Rachel told her what had happened.

"I'll look after James and Charlotte while you go to work," Claire offered.

James and Charlotte were very happy with the idea, having set eyes on Claire's box of biscuits.

Rachel was so grateful that she almost started crying again. Claire gave her a hug and sent her off to work with Steve's redundant packed lunch.

Claire spent the day building dens, making playdough and playing hide-and-seek. She enjoyed it so much that she was taken by surprise when Rachel knocked on her door at the end of the day.

"Is it this late already? Time has flown!" Claire said, a little sadly. She didn't want to say goodbye to the children and never play with them again.

"I'm glad you say that. I've been feeling guilty all day for saddling you with the children."

"You have nothing to feel guilty about! It's been a real pleasure and I'd be more than happy to do it again if you need it."

Rachel hesitated. "That would be very helpful, but I can't take advantage of you like that. I must pay you as a childminder."

Yes, of course, a childminder! This was the perfect job for her! And when Rachel didn't need her, she could look after other children.

"Yes, that's fine," Claire said.

Rachel took her hands in hers and squeezed them. "Thank you so much."

Claire chuckled. "I'm the one who should thank you. You've just helped me work out what job I want to do!"

9. ROOM FOR IMPROVEMENT

"Today you're going to Housekeeping," Liz, the restaurant manager, declared.

Simona looked at her blankly. "Housekeeping" was one of many English words, together with "crumpet", "hash brown" and "hock", that they hadn't taught her at school in Italy.

No wonder that, on her first day, taking the breakfast orders had been such a puzzling ordeal that Simona had been switched to kitchen porter duties immediately after.

Loading and unloading the huge dishwasher hadn't been much easier. She might have coped better if she'd had one at home, or if they had given her some training.

Unfortunately, it was a Saturday and everyone in the kitchen was too busy to show her what to do. By nine o'clock the restaurant had run out of clean bowls.

After such disastrous experiences, leaving the restaurant should have been a relief, but failure was more what she felt.

Simona cursed her English teacher who had taught her how to translate Shakespeare and Coleridge but not how to take breakfast orders in a luxury hotel in the English countryside.

Liz must have seen the confusion on her face because she sighed and ran her hands over her apron.

"You'll clean and tidy the rooms. The housekeeper, Anne, will tell you what to do. Any questions?"

Simona shook her head.

"Off you go. You'll find Anne in the storeroom."

Simona had no idea where the storeroom was, but it would be easier to find it herself than to understand Liz's directions, so she ventured down the maze of corridors.

Where would they send her if she bungled housekeeping too? Were there any other jobs left at the Royal Park Hotel?

She found herself in a little courtyard and the answer materialised in front of her. A cloud of steam and soapy fragrances emanated from a windowless room with the door wide open.

Candyfloss clouds formed outside the door as the hot vapours clashed with the cold air outside. It must be unpleasantly hot inside, because the person feeding crumpled tablecloths into the roller was shirtless and his back gleamed with sweat.

The machine spat out perfectly flat tablecloths and napkins, and the guy rushed to collect, fold and feed them back in.

The place reminded her of a Victorian factory and a solitary confinement cell at the same time.

What with the machines' din and the frantic pace of the work, Simona imagined that there wouldn't be much conversation if she were sent to work with him. Most likely, she'd be sent there to work on her own. In both cases, it would not do her English any good.

The man must have felt that someone was staring at him because he suddenly turned towards her.

Boy, was he handsome! What kind of hotel made gorgeous people work in the dungeons instead of reception?

He pinned her with a pair of blue eyes and something flickered across his face. Simona couldn't tell whether it was anger, embarrassment or a mixture of the two, but it was clear that he wasn't happy to be seen there.

She immediately averted her gaze and was about to resume her search for the storeroom when a woman's voice reached her.

"Hello. Are you the new girl joining us today?"

She had blonde hair, generous curves and a basket full of cleaning products that smelled like limoncello.

"Yes, I'm Simona."

"I'm Rose. Come on, the storeroom is this way."

It was the opposite direction to the one Simona had been about to take, and it was the direction Rose had just come from, which suggested someone had sent Rose to look for her. Thank goodness for that!

***

Jonathan pulled a large tablecloth out of the roller and folded it. The laundry was frantic, noisy and hot, but there was one thing he liked about it. He was alone.

Alone with his thoughts and away from the pointed fingers and whispers of other staff who couldn't understand why a grown man with a posh accent was scrubbing pots and pans instead of sitting in an office.

Only Michael, the hotel manager, knew who he was and why he was doing this.

Jonathan wasn't sure if he understood why he was doing it, but then even his own father—owner and founder of the hotel chain—didn't understand.

"You don't need to work your way up the ranks. I'm stepping down in January and you'll be in charge of the ship," he'd told him.

"It's precisely because I'll be in charge that I must do this and do it now."

How else could he understand the business? He had to experience being a porter, a bell boy, a laundry worker, a housekeeper and a waiter.

Hospitality was a notoriously volatile business, with high staff turnover and, often, low staff welfare.

But he wanted his hotels to be different. He wanted people to work for him because they felt safe, valued and happy there, not because he paid them a few pennies an hour more than his competitors.

To do this, he needed to know what the work felt like, not on paper but on his own skin. He wanted the full experience, warts and all, even if that meant lying to the people he worked with.

At least in the laundry there was no one to ask him questions, trying to peek into his life.

Until this morning, when that pretty dark-haired young woman peered through the door and caught him off-guard and shirtless. After a week of complete solitude, he had almost forgotten that there were other people in the hotel. He must have darted her a less-than-friendly glance, because she'd averted her gaze and turned around.

"Knock, knock," a voice said behind him.

It was Anne, the housekeeper.

It was nice of her to make a noise to avoid startling him. The machines were so loud that you wouldn't notice someone coming up to you otherwise.

"Hello, Anne."

"Hello, Jonathan. The new kitchen porter has cut his arm, got some stitches, and needs to keep his injury dry. Michael thinks that he should take your place in the laundry until he's healed and you should join Housekeeping for a while." Anne paused. "I don't see why you can't do a direct swap with the kitchen porter. You did that job before, and very well too, from what I heard. We would keep your pay the same, of course. But for some mysterious reason, Michael insists that you join housekeeping." She cocked an eyebrow. "Is there something going on?"

Jonathan stiffened. "What do you mean?"

"If you have requested to move to Housekeeping because you've got your eye on one of my girls, you've made a mistake. Any funny business, and I—"

"I have asked to go to Housekeeping, but

you don't need to worry," Jonathan interrupted. "I am not interested in any of your girls."

"Then why?"

It was clear that Anne didn't like a man intruding on her all-female team and that she was going to be suspicious until he gave her a satisfactory reason.

"I just want to have a go at all the jobs there are. So when do I become one of your girls?" He flashed her one of his best smiles.

Anne sighed. "You are just too charming, it's impossible to be a dragon with you. Come to the storeroom tomorrow at nine. And don't make trouble among my girls with smiles like that," she warned him.

***

Rose and Simona wheeled their trolleys, overflowing with clean linen and towels, out of the storeroom and trundled up to their first room.

"Don't worry. You'll be fine," Rose added, as if reading Simona's fear. "I'll show you the ropes."

Simona smiled thankfully and made a mental note to remember where the "ropes" were kept.

Their first room was a changeover, so they had to strip the beds and change all the towels, as well as vacuum, clean the bathrooms and empty the bins.

Stripping the emperor-size bed was no trouble, but putting the new sheets back onto that thick rubbery mattress was a completely different matter.

Rose effortlessly lifted the mattress's corner with one hand and wrapped the sheet around it with the other. However, Simona could only manage to push the fabric in the gap between bed and mattress with her fingers, producing creases that split the bed diagonally in half. Rose showed her again how to do it properly, but it seemed that Simona's biceps just weren't strong enough.

"Perhaps it's better that you leave the beds to me, and you do the vacuuming," Rose suggested after a few unsuccessful attempts.

Simona felt disappointed and deflated until the vacuum cleaner whooshed to life and she felt that she had finally found a job that she could do well.

But although she was vacuuming well, she wasn't doing it fast enough, and Rose was waiting for her.

The bathrooms were even more trouble. There were different cleaning products for the enamel, the marble and the metal fittings, and way too many words for Simona to remember.

The complimentary toiletries were a real minefield, and Simona had to read the labels carefully if she didn't want to put the body lotion in place of the shower gel.

Although they hadn't taken a morning break, when it was time for their lunch break they were well behind schedule and Rose's patience was wearing thin.

"One more room and we'll break for lunch," she said with a sigh.

Simona nodded. She couldn't trust herself to speak without her voice breaking.

When she had left Italy, she had felt like a reasonably capable human being, but now she had started to doubt if there was anything in the world she could do well.

***

The next morning, Simona was pleasantly surprised to be dispatched to Housekeeping again. She couldn't have done too poor a job the day before if they were keeping her. Two days was longer than she had lasted in the kitchen.

As soon as she walked into the room, she clearly felt a vibration of excitement in the air. Then she saw the cause. The handsome laundry man was there.

"Today we are going to trial some new cleaning products," Anne announced. "They're cheaper so the management wants to switch over."

Some of the other housekeepers rolled their eyes. The laundry man clenched his jaw.

"Are you the salesman?" one of the girls asked him.

"No," Rose replied for him. "Jonathan comes from the laundry, but will be working with us for a few days."

Silent excitement rippled through the room like the waves of skimming stone.

"Rose, as you're already showing Simona the ropes, do you mind taking Jonathan with you too?"

An unusual mixture of relief and nerves took over Simona. The guy was uncomfortably handsome, but it would surely be helpful to hear Rose repeat the instructions for him. Perhaps she would finally find out where these elusive ropes were kept.

"Sure," Rose replied, grinning to her ears.

But her grin soon disappeared when it became obvious that Jonathan was as inept as Simona in the housekeeping chores. Strength, height and muscle power were on his side, but he had even less of a clue than Simona about techniques and products.

It was refreshing for Simona not to be alone in her predicament, and she felt a companionable sympathy for him.

"It's not as easy as it looks," he said to her, tongue between his teeth with the effort of tying a bow on the complimentary box of chocolates.

"Especially when you don't know the language and have trouble understanding the instructions," she confessed more candidly than she had intended.

"Your English is not bad," he replied. "I wish my Italian was as good as your English! Is this why you are here?"

"Yes. I've just finished my Biochemistry PhD and I've struggled a lot at science conferences because of my poor English, so I decided to take a year out to knock the problem on the… heels?"

He smiled. "On the head would be better."

Simona felt her cheeks flush but she wasn't sure whether it was because of her mistake or that irresistible smile.

Then she noticed that he was applying the toilet cleaning spray onto the glass.

"You shouldn't use that on the window," she said, handing him the window spray.

He glanced at the labels. "Oh, dear. Thanks."

A couple of minutes later, he started coughing.

There was a strangled quality to that sound, so Simona stopped polishing the desk and turned around.

Jonathan's face was red and his eyes were watering.

She rushed up to him. "Are you all right?"

"Crikey, what's in this stuff?" he wheezed.

Simona checked the ingredients on the bottle of glass cleaner. It contained a chemical that she had worked with. Her research had shown that it could cause respiratory problems for some people.

"What's the matter?" Rose asked, emerging from the ensuite bathroom.

"Quick, call an ambulance!" Simona told her, yanking the window open to let in fresh air. Then she turned to Jonathan. "Wash your hands!"

He turned his blotchy face to her with a look of complete trust and did what she had asked.

Then she led him outside, where the ambulance reached them in a couple of minutes. Simona told the paramedics what had happened and what drugs might help. She had no trouble with scientific terms in English.

The ambulance whisked Jonathan away and Simona watched it disappear, wondering if she should have asked to go with him.

***

The next day, Simona's heart sank when she found that Jonathan wasn't at the morning briefing.

She tried to convince herself that she was just worried for his health, and not sad about not seeing him again.

"Jonathan is recovering well," Anne informed everyone, "but he won't be joining us today. Now, before we start on the rooms, there's a staff meeting in the orangery."

As she followed her colleagues out of the storeroom and through the maze of corridors, Simona couldn't help feeling apprehensive.

Was this meeting in some way connected with Jonathan's accident? Had he got into trouble over it? She sincerely hoped not.

The orangery was buzzing with hushed speculations. Perhaps everyone else was as puzzled and apprehensive as her.

The grounds staff shifted uneasily from one leg to the other in their muddy boots. The kitchen staff emerged from the swing doors like cave dwellers squinting into the sunlight. The receptionist and the managers looked at the seating with uncertainty, probably conscious of a million degrees of hierarchy. Only the waiting staff looked at ease on their home turf.

Simona and the other housekeepers

clustered around Anne and remained standing by the door.

A man in a suit appeared on the steps leading to the garden. He was handsome and expensively dressed.

"Hello, everyone," he said, and silence descended. "I want to thank you all for the terrific job you do for our guests. Now that I have shared your work, even if only for a short time, I can appreciate how hard it is and how skilled you are. The crockery I broke in the kitchen, the napkins I burned in the rotary ironer and the bush in the rose garden that I pruned too brutally bear witness to how difficult I've found your jobs. My sincere apologies. I also need to apologise to the guests who will be staying in room 504," he continued, "where I mistook the toilet cleaner for the window spray."

At that, everyone burst into hearty laughter. But not Simona.

Through the crisp suit, the neat hair, the expensive glasses, she saw him. Jonathan.

What did his speech mean? Who was he? Judging by the murmur that was spreading in the room, everyone was wondering the same.

"By the way, we are going back to the cleaning products we used before," he said, glancing at Anne. "You'll be relieved to hear that I'm returning to the one job I know how to do: director of sales. The kitchen, the laundry, the garden and the housekeeping are much better left to the professionals. Then, in January, I will take the helm from my father, who's retiring, and will become your CEO."

Simona didn't hear the rest of the speech, the congratulations or the exclamations of surprise from the other staff. All she could think was that Jonathan was going to be the top man in the company and there was no way that their paths would ever cross again.

***

Jonathan felt relieved when he had finished his speech and come clean about his identity. He hated lies. But now another tricky task awaited him.

Joanathan had ordered tea and cakes for the staff for after his announcement and, while everyone was enjoying being treated, he looked around for Simona. He saw her in a corner and rushed up to her.

"Hello, Simona. Thank you for what you did yesterday."

"It was just luck that I had worked on that chemical," she answered tensely.

"I meant for pointing out that I was using the toilet cleaner."

Simona laughed and that seemed to break

the tension.

"You've saved my honour, and my life, so I owe you dinner at the very least. Are you free tonight?"

She looked around at the packed room.

"No, not here," Jonathan whispered. "Somewhere else. Just you and me."

***

Based on her Chemistry knowledge, Simona was promoted to Health and Safety Officer and was offered a training course so that she wasn't thrown in at the deep end again.

After the first dinner with Jonathan, others followed. Then came an engagement ring and a wedding bouquet. By then, Simona had learnt to speak English perfectly, also thanks to Jonathan's patience.

But she never found out where the hotel kept those famous ropes.

10. IT'S GOT TO BE PERFECT

Giada was one of those students who excelled at everything: sports, academic subjects, her social life. You name it, she was at the top. And she was kind too, so everybody at school liked her, even if they envied her.

Seeing her as accomplished as that, everyone assumed she must be unshakeably happy. But she wasn't.

As a small child, Giada had been told to reach for the stars, and she had set her eyes on becoming an astronaut.

At primary school, she was told that she could achieve anything she set her mind to, and for a while, she set her mind to becoming a Roman empress.

Now that she was eighteen and about to finish school, Giada had ditched the empress and astronaut ambitions, and settled on becoming a brain surgeon. But only the best brain surgeon in the world would do.

Her grades were already good enough to give her access to medical school, and she was sure to pass the entrance test, but she still wanted to ace her final school exams.

She wasn't as gifted in maths as in her other subjects, but she wanted the top grade in that subject too, so she asked her parents to sign her up for private maths tuition. That's how she met Felicita.

***

Felicita loved maths and people, though not necessarily in this order.

Teaching maths to secondary school pupils had combined her two great loves, so when she retired from her school job, she started giving private maths tuition from the comfort of her beautiful flat in the centre of Pisa.

Most of the pupils who came to her hated maths, found it incomprehensible, and had been sent to her in the hope that Felicita could help them keep afloat in their school studies. These students didn't see the point of studying maths, and believed the world would be a happier place if it didn't exist.

Felicita would show them the world-famous leaning tower out of her window.

"It would be standing straight if the engineers had done their calculations correctly," she'd tell them.

Sometimes her students complained about other subjects too.

"What's the point of studying old novels?" they'd ask.

Then she'd pick up one of her beautiful porcelain ornaments. "What's the point of beauty?" she'd reply.

Occasionally, a different kind of student landed on Felicita's shores: a gifted pupil who wanted to improve their grades.

They were a different kind of challenge for Felicita, but one that she enjoyed all the same.

Giada was one of them. She hadn't come to Felicita to survive maths but to thrive in it. She was a pupil who wanted to soar, and she needed Felicita to help her strengthen her wings.

Giada asked questions that Felicita often had to think hard about or look up somewhere else. Even if Giada got the correct answer by luck, Felicita wouldn't let her move on until she was sure Giada had understood the process.

Felicita and Giada worked hard together all through the academic year, and now that it was exam results day, they would be reaping the rewards.

Like every year, Felicita sat by her landline, waiting for the calls from her pupils, sharing their news. There might be tears of disappointment and frustration for some, while for others there might be tears of happiness and relief. Felicita prayed that everyone got what was good for them, and that they would accept it and learn from the experience.

***

Giada stared at the school's results board, unable to trust her eyes. Had she really got ninety-nine? Just one point short of the top grade? Her parents, her teachers, her classmates—everyone had expected her to get the top mark.

Tears pricked her eyes and her throat felt like she was swallowing glass.

Her mum squeezed her hand. "Don't worry. You'll still get into medical school."

What consolation was that when she was going to be stuck with that almost-but-not-quite-top grade for the rest of her life? It felt like one of Michelangelo's unfinished sculptures, condemned to remain incomplete forever. How could it have happened?

She needed to find out from her teachers what had gone wrong, but right now she needed to have a cry.

"It's a shame. You made a mistake in the last maths question," her teacher explained to her later.

Giada remembered finding that question hard. She had never liked those mathematical functions. Confronted with it, she had feared not getting the top grade and had panicked.

"I always struggle with those functions. My mind went blank," she confessed.

"You can't excel at everything," her teacher said benignly.

Why couldn't she? All through her life, she had. This was so confusing. Since she was a child, everyone had told her to aim for the stars. Yet now that she hadn't quite reached, and had landed on a cloud instead, her teacher and her mum were telling her that it was just fine.

***

The first phone call Felicita received was from a pupil who had struggled in maths so much that Felicita had suggested he repeat the year. The boy had rejected the suggestion and Felicita had been on tenterhooks since.

"Hello, Miss Felicita, it's me."

He sounded pleased but Felicita didn't want to sing victory too soon. Even if it would prove her wrong, she wanted him to pass with all her heart.

"How did it go?" She tried not to sound too anxious.

"I passed!"

Felicita whooped, and a few minutes later the boy and his parents were at her door with a bunch of flowers and happy tears in their eyes.

Next was another student who got exactly what Felicita had expected, and he was happy.

Another pupil got a lower grade than expected but she wasn't upset.

One after another, all of Felicita's other students gave her their news, until there was no one left but Giada.

Felicita was getting worried when, finally, her doorbell rang.

"Oh, dear," Felicita said at the sight of a puffy-eyed Giada.

As soon as she stepped into the flat, the girl threw herself into Felicita's arms.

"What happened?" Felicita asked, patting Giada's back soothingly.

Things must have gone very wrong to get Giada into such a state.

Felicita led Giada to a chair and offered her a glass of water.

When Giada was finally able to talk, she turned to her tutor.

"I made a mistake in the question about functions and I got ninety-nine."

"Pardon?" Felicita thought that she must have heard wrong.

Giada squirmed, as if repeating her score was painful. "I got ninety-nine."

"It's just one point less than the top grade."

"Exactly! And I needed the top grade." Giada burst into sobs again.

"Needed? What for?"

"I wanted it."

Felicita took a pen and a pad of paper and sat next to Giada.

"We're going to have one last maths lesson."

"There's no point showing me where I went wrong in the exam. It's too late," Giada replied with a sniffle.

"I'm not. I'm showing you where you're going wrong now."

Felicita wrote down an equation, but instead of letters and numbers, it was made of words.

"Happiness equals what you've got minus what you want. You can make happiness bigger by having more, or by wanting less. Which do you think is easier to do?" she asked.

"Making 'what you want' smaller."

"I agree." Felicita nodded. "People try to achieve happiness by increasing what they have, but that's the one thing that's not under their control. You can rarely change what you have, but you can usually change what you want."

Giada looked down. "What about reaching

for the stars? Aiming high?"

Felicita smiled. "Stars are burning hot. Do you remember the story of Icarus, who plummeted to his death after flying too close to the sun on wings made of feathers and wax?"

Giada nodded. "Yes, but Icarus had been told not to fly too low, or the foam of the sea would soak the feathers of his wings," Giada pointed out.

"Yes. So we have to fly somewhere in between, not too high and not too low. We each need to find the right height for us."

Giada nodded and blew her nose.

***

In September, Giada enrolled at medical school and eventually became a brain surgeon, though not a world-famous one.

Every now and then, she still wondered what it might feel like to be the best brain surgeon in the world, but most of the times she was happy just to make other people's lives better.

The End

Other books by Stefania Hartley

Short Stories Collections:

A Quiet Life
Sweet Surprises
The Season to Be Jolly
Sand, Sea & Tamburello
To Be Loved
Drive Me Crazy
A Season of Goodwill
What's Yours is Mine
Stars Are Silver
A Slip of the Tongue
Confetti and Lemon Blossom
Fresh from the Sea

Good Habits
Welcome to Quayside
Tales from the Parish

Short Romances:

How to Choose a Husband
The Italian Fake Date
Sweet Competition for Camillo's Café
Second Chances at Mamma's Trattoria
Under Far Eastern Skies

Cosy Mysteries:

Father Roberto and the Missing Money
Father Roberto and the Runaway Ring
Father Roberto and the Rural Riots
Father Roberto and the Mystery of the Microscope
Father Roberto and the Commotion at the Catacombs

ABOUT THE AUTHOR

Stefania was born in Sicily and immediately started growing, but not very much. She left her sunny island after falling head over heels in love with an Englishman, and now she lives in the UK with her husband and their three children. Having finally learnt English, she's enjoying it so much that she now writes novels and short stories which have been longlisted, shortlisted, commended, and won prizes.

She'd love you to leave a review and to sign up for her newsletter so she can let you know when a new book is out and send you an exclusive short story:

www.stefaniahartley.com/subscribe

www.ingramcontent.com/pod-product-compliance
Lightning Source LLC
LaVergne TN
LVHW020048110826
845155LV00029B/690

* 9 7 8 1 9 1 4 6 0 6 5 3 3 *